JAMMER STAR

orca sports

JAMMER STAR

KATE HARGREAVES

ORCA BOOK PUBLISHERS

Library and Archives Canada Cataloguing in Publication

Hargreaves, Kate, author
Jammer star / Kate Hargreaves.
(Orca sports)

Issued in print and electronic formats.
ISBN 978-1-4598-1718-0 (SOFTCOVER).—ISBN 978-1-4598-1719-7 (PDF).—
ISBN 978-1-4598-1720-3 (EPUB)

I. Title. II. Series: Orca sports
PS8615.A727J36 2019   jc813'.6   C2018-904769-0
                         C2018-904770-4

First published in the United States, 2019
Library of Congress Control Number: 2018952762

Summary: In this high-interest sports novel for young readers,
Robin desperately wants to be the MVP for her roller-derby team.

*Orca Book Publishers is dedicated to preserving the environment and
has printed this book on Forest Stewardship Council® certified paper.*

Orca Book Publishers gratefully acknowledges the support for its publishing
programs provided by the following agencies: the Government of Canada,
the Canada Council for the Arts and the Province of British Columbia
through the BC Arts Council and the Book Publishing Tax Credit.

Edited by Tanya Trafford
Cover photography by joe mac/midnight matinee
Author photo by Every Little Wonder Photography (Sarah Kivell)

ORCA BOOK PUBLISHERS
orcabook.com

Printed and bound in Canada.

22 21 20 19 • 4 3 2 1

For Winn

Chapter One

Knees bent, legs loaded like springs. Your toe-stop rests on the jammer line. You time your breaths to stay in control: in, out, in, out. Focus, Robin. Look *through* the blockers to where you want to go. Fix your stare down the track, past the pivot line, around the apex. Whatever you do, don't look those blockers in the eye. Don't show them any fear. Don't let your hands shake while you wait for the start whistle.

Out of the corner of your eye, you see the green jammer next to you fidget on her skates. She moves side to side, hopping up on her toe-stops and back down again. Don't let her distract you. Focus.

"Five seconds!" the jam timer yells and holds her whistle to her mouth. You ease into an even lower stance. Your pivot turns around and nods in your direction. You're ready. You know what to do. Your wall knows what to do.

Screeeeeee! The jam timer's whistle cuts through the arena as she drops her arm to start the jam.

You blast forward, crashing your shoulder and hip into a seam in the wall of green blockers, and push hard. You can hear your blockers behind you calling out the green jammer's position. "Inside! Outside! Out of bounds! Down!" They've got her, and you have time to escape! You lay a big hit on the green blocker holding the outside line. She slides out of bounds. You burst through the hole in her wall before it closes and duck a last-ditch hit from the green captain.

As you clear the pack, you hear two whistles. Lead jammer! The track opens up ahead of you, and you skate low, calm, controlled. Your crossovers are smooth and efficient. They're going to look great in photos after the bout, but that doesn't matter. Right now, you've got to get back to the pack and score some points for your team.

Fifteen feet behind the pack and gaining on them fast, you hear your teammate shout, "She's out!" The green jammer has danced around your team on the inside line and escaped. She's far enough behind you that you still have a chance to pass some green blockers and score. But the inside line is obstructed by a tall green blocker you *know* you can't move out of the way. The center of the pack is on lockdown too, blockers pressed together, bracing for your hit. And the outside line? Well, that's just dangerous.

Just as you start to check your speed, your pivot calls, "Outside!" You know you have to seize your chance *now*. There's less than a foot of space, but you jump up on your toe-stops and hop your way through the danger and into the safety of the open track.

3

The jam referee raises her hand. Four points!

"Call it off, Robin!" You tap your hips twice just as the green jammer nears the pack. The referees blow their whistles. The jam is over, score 4-0!

"Great job, Robin!" The coach slaps you on the back as you slide onto the bench for some water. "What a jam!"

"*Well, folks, it looks like we've got our* MVP *for the game! Robiiiiin CookieJaarrrrs!*"

You roll over to the announcer's table and accept the huge trophy. Your teammates surround you in a mass of sweaty purple jerseys and smiling faces. They're cheering your name!

"Robin! Robin! Robin!"

"Robin!"

"Huh?" I shake my head and look up at Coach Queenie.

"Robin, snap out of it! You're jamming next. I need you to get your head in the game." Queenie points at the track. "You know, *this* game. Roller derby?"

"What? Oh. Sorry, Coach. I was trying to do positive visualization."

"That's great, Robin. I know we've been talking about mental game at practice. But now I need you to take your positive visualization and turn it into some positive game-play on the track."

Coach Queenie tosses me the jammer cover, and I snap the elastic cover over my helmet. *Gulp.* My first jam of the game, and all the visualization in the world isn't going to get me past those mean green blockers any more easily.

"Remember, Robin, it's not just you out there. You've got four blockers all working with you."

A whistle blasts and a referee yells across the arena, "Purple seven two, multi-player block!"

"Okay, make that three blockers until 72 gets out of the penalty box," Queenie says with a frown. "Trust yourself and your own skating style. Stay away from the edges, look for help from your teammates, and don't give up! You've got this."

"Okay. I'm going to do my best."

"That's all I ask for. Now go get 'em, jammer girl!"

Coach Queenie taps the star on the side of my helmet. Right. I'm the jammer. I have a team to help me. I have my own jamming style. Coach wouldn't ask me to jam if she didn't think I could.

Four whistle blasts ring through the arena. It's my turn to get out on the track.

I glide toward the jam line, and *ouch!* Somehow I'm on the floor already. The jam hasn't even started, and I'm already down.

"Watch out for the rope! It's the fifth blocker, you know!" The green jammer offers me a hand up. Her long braids swing out from under her helmet. I can feel my ears growing red and warm. I mutter, "I'm fine" and pull myself back onto my feet.

"In this, the ninth jam of the first half, we have a new face on the jammer line for the Creek City Juniors."

Jim the Announcer Guy's voice cuts through the cheering parents in the arena.

"*In purple, we've got number 13, Robiiiiiin CoooookieJaaaaaars, squaring up against Uptown Junior Crushers number 44, Zippy Loooooooongstockings.*"

Zippy waves to the audience and the announcer's words start to sink in. Robin CookieJars, that's me. This is my jam. My chance to prove I can really do this!

"Five seconds!"

Focus, breathe—okay, let's go.

Screee! The jam-start whistle blows, and before I can even remember to move, Zippy has scooted along the inside line and is dancing back and forth behind my wall of blockers.

"Robin, go!" Coach Queenie calls from the bench.

I tuck my shoulder and push hard into the wall of green blockers like I did in my daydream. But this time they don't budge. Instead, I lose my balance again. My kneepads clatter against the concrete. The audience *oohs*.

"A solid Uptown wall sends Creek City jammer Robin CookieJars flying. Zippy Longstockings picks up lead jammer status!"

Damn! No lead means Zippy is in control of this jam. I'm not even out of the pack yet. I take a step back and try a different spot in the wall, pushing my hip against the inside blocker. But her teammate appears out of nowhere and sweeps me off the track and back onto the ground. My legs burn as I pull myself up and rush back onto the track. Zippy blurs past. In all the confusion, she finds a hole in the purple wall up ahead.

"That's a grand slam! Five points go to Zippy Longstockings!"

I'm still stuck, and Zippy is stealing all the points! I have to get out. Queenie's advice rings in my head, to play *my* game. Pushing toward the middle of their wall, I make my way up the track inch by inch until I'm able to build some momentum.

"Zoom! She sure is zippy! Uptown picks up another five points as Robin CookieJars continues to fight hard!"

"Push, Robin, push!" Queenie calls from the bench. Zippy squeaks past again. *I'm trying!* I can't even gasp out the words as I puff and pant behind the superhuman wall of green.

Four whistles save me. I roll back over to the bench, grab my water and fight to push down the lump that is creeping up my throat. *There's no crying in derby. There's no crying in derby. Pull it together, Robin.*

"It's okay," says Coach Queenie. "Those are some tough blockers, and you did your best." She snaps the jammer cover off my helmet and heads back down the bench.

"Tough? They're frigging impossible!"

"With a hop, skip and a beautiful spin on the inside line, it looks like purple jammer April Powers is in the lead and heading back in for her scoring pass!"

The bench erupts around me. "Go, April!"

Kat N. Crunch taps me on the shoulder and points at the track. "Did you see that, Robin? April is so awesome! She's going to get us back in this game!"

Out on the track, April Powers is a flash of blond ponytail and willowy limbs. She dances and spins through the pack.

"That's five points, a grand slam for Creek City's April Powers!"

The audience roars. "April! April!"

I take a long gulp from my water bottle and sigh. So much for impossible.

Chapter Two

"April Powers is closing the score gap. Those green Crushers are looking pretty worried as she rounds the track for her next pass!"

Could April Powers *be* any more perfect? She slips through gaps that don't even exist while I'm panting and pushing and getting nowhere. She jumps and spins and crosses over like she's dancing, not playing a contact sport. She *always* looks amazing in derby photos, because somehow she doesn't bother to break a sweat. And she is always, *always* MVP.

The clock is ticking for the end of the two-minute jam. April has already racked up twenty points. She's set to pick up five more before the whistles sound. There's a tiny hole on the inside line that no one could make it through. Except April. The other team probably doesn't even think anyone would try. The track edges are lava—that's what Queenie says—but somehow April never gets burned.

With five seconds to go, April hurtles toward the gap, and for a bright moment it seems as if the big, tall, mean-looking girl in green doesn't see her coming. That is, until she closes the door on April's easy path through the pack. All it takes is one step to close off the line, and *thunk!*

I've never seen April take a hit like that. I barely see April get hit *at all*. Her foot-work and timing are so good that she tends to dodge blockers without them even making contact. This time is different. April flies across the inside line and crumples in the ref lane. Everyone on the track stops skating, and the arena falls silent.

The referees whistle the jam dead. April rolls onto her back, breathing hard. She does not get up.

"Medics! Medics!"

April pulls herself up to sitting as Coach Queenie sprints to the inside track, waving the medics over.

With Queenie's shoulder under her arm, April rises to her feet and rolls off the track, brushing the dust off her tights. She waves the medics off as they try to follow her to the bench, blood-pressure gauge and clipboard in hand.

"I'm fine, I'm fine!"

A long, sweeping whistle signals half-time. The skaters clear the benches and head for the dressing rooms.

April pulls off her helmet and, before anyone can insist on a checkup, skates out the back Zamboni door.

"She probably just needs a little air," Coach Queenie says. "Everyone else to the dressing room. Robin..." She turns to me as I start skating away, "Can I talk to you for a second?"

It must be about my awful jam. April gets twenty points, and I get lapped four times. Maybe I'm getting benched for the rest of the game. I wouldn't blame Coach for benching me for the rest of the season.

"Listen, Robin, I know April says she's okay, but that was a pretty nasty hit. I need you to be ready to jam in the second half if April isn't feeling up to it. Okay?"

"But I was the worst, Coach! I didn't get through at all. I don't have the footwork April does. I can't do it."

"Everyone has their own style. Not everyone gets by on footwork and fancy stuff. Don't try to be April—just be you. You'll be great."

"So I'm not benched?"

"No way, jammer girl, we need you!" said Coach. "Now go get yourself a banana or something, because this is going to be a tough second half."

Jammer girl. She called me jammer again. She said they need me. My team needs me. To jam. I will get a second chance to prove myself. But can I?

"I think I need more than a banana to get through that wall!" I yell at Queenie's back as she heads outside and toward our winded superstar.

"Then I suggest you make it two bananas, jammer girl!" she yells back.

Chapter Three

"You sure you're good to go, April?"

"I told you, I'm fine." April snatches the jammer cover from Queenie's outstretched hand and sets her focus on the track. She seems a bit paler than usual. And her eyes are a little red, like she's been crying.

"Hey, April!"

Nothing.

"Hey, April!" I yell louder. I'm only three seats down from her on the bench. She ignores me. Maybe she's doing her own positive visualization. Does April Powers even need to? She must know she's the best.

She's probably got a whole room of MVP trophies at home to remind her. "Hey, April, I think you're going to be great out there," I mutter. Who cares if she hears me or not?

The whistle to end half-time rings through the arena. April tugs the jammer cover over her helmet and heads for the line. *April doesn't trip on the rope.* That's a rookie mistake. Maybe when I've been playing for as long as she has I won't make such an idiot of myself. So only a few more years of stupid falls and embarrassment to go.

The jam-start whistle blows, and April jumps off the line, heading for an impossibly small hole on the outside. It's risky, as usual, but this is April. With her fancy feet, she can get through anything.

"Ohhhh! And Uptown closes up the outside line, cutting off April Powers for what I believe is only the second time this evening!"

Two whistle blasts signal lead jammer, but April's still in the pack, dancing back and forth behind a solid green wall. Wait a second. April isn't lead?

17

April spins off the inside blocker and tries to find a hole in the middle of the wall, but they seal up any cracks too fast for her to breach. The same wall of green that I faced. The impossible, super-strong team that just wouldn't let me through. They weren't a problem for April before, but now she's totally stuck.

"Push, April! Come on, girl!" Queenie's forehead wrinkles as she squints across the track. She's not hiding her confusion. She's used to seeing April squeak past even the meanest, biggest, strongest blockers. I'm not sure she even knows what to say to help April out. Usually it's all "Great job, April!" and "Awesome jam, Powers!"

"Another grand slam for Uptown in green!"

Over and over, the green jammer laps the pack as our team scrambles to help April get through. She's sweating, panting and slowing down. Lining herself up behind the wall, April grimaces as she pushes, but no one moves.

"We got her, girls!" the green pivot calls out, grinning. "She's tired. We can hold her."

Since I started skating with Creek City Junior Derby last year, I don't think I've *ever* seen April tired. Endurance laps around the track? She breezes through. The dreaded twenty-seven laps in five minutes? April racks up thirty-three and barely even needs a sip of water after. Even against our coaches during practice, she never looks frazzled. And they block for the adult Creek City league! No drill, skill and especially no blocker gets the better of April.

And yet tonight, out on the track, against boring old Uptown Junior Crushers, April is sliding onto the concrete floor again and again. And she is pulling herself up slower and slower each time. The jam ends, and Queenie calls a time-out, waving the assistant coach over from turn three. April barely rolls herself to the end of the bench and drops onto the seat, breathing hard. Our whole team shifts over to give her space. No one wants to ask April what's wrong.

If she's okay. That would be admitting that something is seriously up with our superstar jammer. April wipes her bangs off her sweaty forehead and gulps from her water bottle, spilling onto the floor.

"Okay, so I think we'll sub in Robin. I think she's got the push we need right now." Queenie is talking in a low whisper, huddled over her clipboard.

Did she just say what I think she did? If April can't beat these blockers, how do I stand a chance?

Queenie tosses me the jammer cover. I turn it over in my hands before sliding it over my helmet. *Focus.* This time, not even the track boundary rope is going to trip me up.

There's no time for positive visualization, so I repeat Queenie's advice to myself: *down the middle, push hard, trust your team, don't give up.* I ready my shoulder into a seam in the green wall as the tall blocker catches my eye and grins.

"Five seconds!" *Scree!*

They're moving! The wall is moving, and my team has the green jammer on lockdown. I push hard down the middle. *Nothing fancy, Robin.* The green wall rolls faster and faster away from my team, and I hear a referee yell, "No pack!" Suddenly I'm out of the pack and skating my lap, on my way to score points. Is that jam referee pointing at me? I'm lead!

The green jammer—I think it's that Zippy girl again—is on my tail, and I've got to hurry if I'm going to get any points. I rush into the pack, making sure my hit is legal. I pass two of their blockers and tap my hands to my hips. Two points for me and none for Zippy! Success!

With April still resting at the end of the bench and looking a little green in the face, Queenie sends me out to jam more and more in the second half. I'm not creating miracles, but I stay away from the edges. I push hard and low against the green walls, enough to make space for me to get out of the pack and pick up points. I even get lead jammer a couple more times! *This* is what Queenie meant by playing my own style!

As we head into the last jam of the game, Coach Queenie paces the length of the bench, biting her bottom lip. She's holding the jammer cover with a star on each side in one hand and tapping her pen to her clipboard. We're only two points behind. She stops in front of me for a second, checks the scoreboard again and pauses.

"Are you ready to win this game for us?"

Chapter Four

April grabs the cover from Queenie and pulls it onto her helmet.

How could Queenie give the cover to April? I've been getting through! I've been getting points! Why doesn't she trust me to win the game? When she paused in front of me on the bench, my heart almost stopped. But then Queenie changed her mind and handed it to April.

As if she can hear me thinking, Queenie pats me on the shoulder. "You're doing great, Robin, but April's got more experience under pressure. You've really rocked this game tonight. Thanks for stepping up for us and being such a great teammate."

I can feel that lump rising in my throat again. I've been doing my best and it still isn't good enough. Queenie doesn't trust me to win the game for the team. No one gets MVP for being a great teammate.

On the track the jam is on, and April's stuck again, moving slower than ever. Zippy is lead for Uptown and already heading back into the pack for a scoring pass. *See, Queenie? I could have got through!* My teammates are leaning forward on the bench, pushing April to keep trying. "Go, April. Yay, I guess," I mutter at the ground.

Sure, I want our team to win and all, but I find myself willing April to fail. Every misstep she takes, every hit an Uptown blocker lays on her, I have to hold in my grin. April should have to try once in a while. She should know what it feels like to get locked into a wall. To work your hardest but keep getting stuck. To take hit after hit. To watch someone else take home the MVP trophy.

A whistle sends the green jammer to the penalty box. Coach Queenie yells, "POWER JAM!"

Our blockers rush into action, no longer having to worry about preventing the green jammer from breaking out of the pack. They sweep blockers out of April's way and open up a hole just big enough for her to dart through. With a push from our pivot, April is out and heading toward scoring points. But she still has to break through the pack again.

There's no way we're going to win this. We were two points down at the beginning of the jam. And the green jammer picked up two more before going to the box. With ten seconds left, April needs all five points to win the game. A complete grand slam.

Skating her solo lap toward the pack, April is clearly exhausted. She will need way more force than that to push those blockers. My ears warm up. I can't believe I'm so excited to watch us lose.

As the clock ticks down, I grab my water bottle from under my seat, ready to head back to the change room. Game over. We lose. Too bad.

"Jump!" Coach Queenie screams from the bench.

With two seconds left on the clock, April leaps into the air and gracefully clears the entire Uptown team. Four whistles end the jam.

The ref puts an open hand in the air. Five points, grand slam!

"And with that amazing last-second apex jump, it looks like April Powers of Creek City Junior Derby has won the game for her team!"

Queenie and the rest of the team rush to center track to swarm a panting, very pale April with hugs. I linger on the sidelines, waiting for the all-important end-of-game announcement.

"Stick around, folks. In a few minutes we will be announcing the MVPs for the game."

One jump. It was one frigging jump. They couldn't possibly name April MVP for that, could they?

Chapter Five

"*We know that all our skaters worked their very hardest out there tonight, so let's give them a big hand!*"

Come on, Jim, get to the point! Queenie taps me on the shoulder. Not now! I need to hear this announcement.

"Robin, no matter what happens, you did an amazing job today! You followed my direction and really helped the team pull through."

"*I'm happy to announce our Uptown MVP blocker...*"

Ugh, Coach, please! Our team is going to be up next.

"Thanks, Coach. I appreciate it, but—"

"I think you showed a lot of potential, and we can work on really developing your jamming..."

Queenie wants to talk about my game-play strategy, but she's drowning out the announcer. It looks like that tall girl from Uptown picked up MVP blocker. It makes sense, because man, did she ever cover that inside line.

"*The Uptown MVP jammer is...*"

"I'm going to talk to Hurricane Amy about getting you some extra track time. Maybe you can help coach the littles team—"

Great, Queenie, but why are you still *talking? Why now?* Zippy, the girl with the braids, skates up to grab her trophy. No big surprise there. That girl is *fast.*

"*And for your hometown team, your MVP blocker—*"

"Oh, great! Woo-hoo! Good job, Kat!" Queenie cheers as Kat N. Crunch skates forward to pick up her trophy and high-fives the Uptown winners.

"*Aaaaaand... no surprise here after that amazing second-half comeback...*"

Robin CookieJars, right? Me? Finally, it has to be me! I worked so hard against those blockers. I *was* that comeback!

"*And that incredible last-second apex jump!*"

Wait, what?

"*That's right, with her fourteenth consecutive* MVP *win for Creek City Junior Derby, it's Aaaaaapril Poooowwweeeeerrrrrs!*"

The lump crawls back up my throat. I scrunch up my face and bite my lip to push it back down. *No crying in derby. No crying in derby.*

"Where's April?" Queenie asks. The announcer is holding out her trophy, scanning the arena.

"*Well, we'll get this to April later, but let's get our other* MVP *winners together for a group photo!*"

The waterworks are still threatening, so I grab my water bottle and bolt for the dressing room. The door swings open, and I almost fall through it.

"Oh, sorry!" April, gear bag over one shoulder, a baseball cap pulled down over her face, dodges around me. "Hey, you got MVP. They're taking a photo."

Be a good teammate, Robin, come on.

"You were awesome out there! That jump!" I add.

"Oh, okay, yeah, that's cool—can you grab the trophy for me? I've got somewhere I need to be."

"You're not coming to the pancake party?"

"Sorry, not hungry. Just bring the trophy to practice. Or don't. I have a bunch of them anyway. You can keep it if you want." April slings her bag onto her other shoulder and strides out toward the arena doors.

Not hungry? Seriously? I could eat forty pancakes right now. Just the thought of maple syrup and whipped cream is making my stomach grumble.

"Robin, are you in there? We're leaving for Pancake Hut in five!" Queenie's voice echoes across the change room.

"Coming!"

I whip off my protective gear and shove the damp, stinky pads into my backpack. I tie my laces together and throw my skates over my other shoulder. As I head toward the parking lot, I hear Queenie leaning on her horn.

"Robin, let's go!" she calls out her open window.

My stomach rumbles again, maybe louder than the horn.

"Hey, wait!" A voice I recognize very well. "It's Robin, right?"

I look back and see Jim the Announcer Guy holding a trophy. MVP JAMMER is emblazoned across a recycled derby wheel.

"Yes. Hi," I say.

"April never collected this. Can you see that she gets it?"

I could just take the trophy, put it up on my shelf at home and pretend it's mine. April said I could.

"Sorry, my hands are full," I tell him. I'll earn my own damn trophy.

Chapter Six

Okay, so maybe ten pancakes was not such a great idea.

"Hey, Superstar, what about dinner?"

"I'm good, Mom, thanks!" I had to push myself stair by stair to even get *to* my room. Now that the pancakes have settled in my stomach, I don't think I'm going to be able to get out of my computer chair ever again. My legs are noodles, and I've got that sleepy bulging-belly feeling.

"Are you going to come and tell me about your game or what?"

"It was good, Mom, it's cool."

I know my mom wishes she could make it to more of my games. She would love to be there with a sign and noisemakers like some of the other parents, but being on-call for work every weekend makes it hard for her to do anything fun. She gives me a lift here and there, but I don't think she's ever actually seen me play a game. She'd probably hate watching her little girl getting bashed left and right, falling all over the place. A split lip from a stray elbow. A bloody nose every now and then. It's probably better she doesn't watch.

I'm nestled in my chair, cross-legged and wrapped in a blanket. I boot up the old desktop computer and wait for what feels like four hours for it to load. Mom says maybe we can start saving up for a laptop for when I go to college. If I can keep my grades above a B minus. But college is a couple of years away. For now, I'm stuck with this clunker that can pretty much only do word processing and internet surfing.

Luckily, surfing is good enough for what I have planned tonight—a bit of roller-derby research. Maybe it was the power of pancakes or maybe it was chatting with Queenie over our postgame feast that got me out of my rut. MVP or not, I'm feeling more committed to upping my game than ever. Queenie's right—*You got this, jammer girl.*

Permanent marker smudges across my arm. Queenie laughed as I jotted notes on my skin. "I could have given you a piece of paper!"

"It's okay, Coach! I'm making a plan!" I told her. "What do you think?"

–endurance, cross-training

–mental game

–footwork!

"I've got another one. Do you have enough space, or do you need to start on the other arm?" Queenie asks with a laugh. "Roller-derby idols. People you look up to. When I'm feeling down about my game-play, sometimes I like to read interviews with skaters I admire. They have the same struggles. Chatting with a teammate about shared goals and plans is good too."

Easy enough for Queenie to say. She's got a teammate as close as her own house. Coach Quinoa Queen, Queenie for short, and her wife, Hurricane Amy, both play for Creek City's adult team. I bet the conversation in their house is all derby all the time. Queenie doesn't have to worry about talking too much about offensive strategy and the newest skate technology, and Amy doesn't panic about spending hours and hours at practice. Instead of bringing their daughter to dance class or soccer, Amy carts Mean Sprout along to littles derby and gets the whole family involved. Queenie is *totally* living the dream.

Plus, and this a big plus, Queenie and Amy skate on the same team as *the* best skater ever, Annie Mossity. My coaches get to be *friends* with one of the top-ranked skaters in the entire country! I don't even know what I would do if Annie said two words to me, let alone wanted to talk about our shared goals and struggles. I'd probably faint.

The browser finally loads, and without thinking about it I click on the link to my pin board. My home page floods with clothes sites and makeup tutorials pinned by girls from school. There's some cute pets and celebrity boys in the mix, but I click past all that to get to my one and only pin board: Derby Derby Derby!

What can I say? When I like something, I like it. A lot. I've been pinning to this derby board since I first decided to join Creek City Junior Derby last year. So far I've collected more than 200 of my favorite roller-derby pictures and articles.

Last winter Mom took me to the Creek City holiday parade, even though fifteen is *way* too old to be catching candy from people in elf costumes. But it was a Tuesday, and Mom had the night off work, so there we were. Amid all the dancing snowflakes, dogs dressed as reindeer, and marching bands, I spotted some of the coolest-looking women I'd ever seen. And not one of them was dressed like an elf.

They were all different—women with purple hair or tattoos, some tall, some short, some big, some gangly. There were a few who looked old enough to be at college. Probably studying something edgy like rock-music theory and running the campus radio station. There was also a bunch who kind of looked like my mom. And some of them even looked like me! Or, at least, like they could be in my grade.

Behind a big banner that said *Creek City Roller Derby*, these supercool girls were spinning and jumping and gliding around on roller skates. They laughed and waved as they leaped over each other, hip checking, running on their toes and skating backward, all on these cool, old-fashioned-looking quad skates.

"Hi, I'm April. Come join us at Creek City Junior Roller Derby this winter!" A tall girl who looked a couple of years older than me pushed a flyer and a candy cane into my hand and then skated back into the crowd. *Intro to Junior Roller Derby.* "Mom...can I?"

Somehow I convinced my mom that roller derby would be good for me socially, or something. And I guess that's how I ended up here, at nine forty-five at night, full of pancakes and motivation, devouring all the derby information I could find online.

That first month I had tried to quit every single practice. My mom would pull up in the car to pick me up, and before we'd even left the parking lot, the tears would start to flow. *I'm no good. I can barely stand. I can't stop. The other girls are so much better.*

"You wanted to do this, Robin, and not being a natural is no reason to quit. Do you think it was easy learning to be a paramedic? I cried all through school. When you're not a natural at something, you have to try twice as hard. But it's worth it. That's the only way you find out what you're really capable of."

I stuck it out. Even though every T-stop or plow stop or crossover that April demonstrated with so much easy grace was a clatter of pads on concrete for me. I fell down more times than I could count. But finally something clicked.

"Did you know April used to be a figure skater?" Quinoa Queen told me as I picked myself off the ground and rubbed the bruise on my butt for the millionth time. "No one picks it up as fast as she did."

Derby is what really got me into pinning. Every new skill we learned, I searched out on the best derby blogs. I wanted to learn the sneaky tips and tricks before I came back to practice. Where do I put the pressure on my skates? What leg is the best for balance? Do I need to try a different direction? Sure, I'd never show up flawless, like April, but I'd be a hell of a lot better than the week before.

At the top of my pin-board suggestions there's a link to Annie Mossity's blog. An animated gif plays over and over: Annie, powerful and fierce, leaping clear over a rival blocker's butt during last season's playoffs. In two years I'm going to be old enough to try out for Annie's team. But I'm nowhere near that level. I can barely jump a cone. How am I ever going to get to play beside her?

I stick a pin in the article for another day. From what Queenie said, I need a plan that's bigger than one flashy move.

I begin to type:

Robin's Secret MVP *Super Training Plan*
-get to practice early (no getting stuck online. Practice = research)
-go jogging once a week (ugh, endurance. Gotta do it.)
-carry healthy snacks (eat every couple hours for energy. Almonds, bananas, etc.)
-don't go to bed too late (no more late-night pinning!)
-visualize success (working on this one for sure)

I had better get started. First step, getting off the computer and going to sleep. *I got this, Annie. I'm going to play on your team one day.*

Tucked in bed, there's no crowd noise or coaches yelling. Just me making my lap around the track back to the pack, looking for a way to break through and get as many points as I can. The pack lines up just on the apex. I leap high into the air, over the blockers, and land a fabulous game-winning jump.

There is a crowd, and it's roaring.

Chapter Seven

"Mom, derby starts early tonight. Can you drop me off before five?"

We pull into the gravel lot outside the arena at 4:45.

"Are you sure, Robin? Doesn't look like anyone's here yet." My mom scans the parking lot for other skaters and parents.

"Yeah, I'm sure. It's a special jammer practice." I just said that so Mom will let me out. I am here early to get working on my plan. "See, April's car is already here."

April's green hatchback is unmistakable with its roller-skate decal in the back window. This, apparently, is proof enough for my mom. I hop out and she pulls away.

"Pick you up at eight!" she yells out the window.

Why *is* April already here? Sure, I've never shown up for practice this early, but what exactly is she doing here? The car windows are tinted, but I peer in the driver's side. No April. But I think that's her derby bag in the back seat. The arena doors are always locked until Queenie rolls up, so where the heck is she?

Crunch, crunch, crunch, crunch.

Footfalls in the gravel. April rounds the corner of the arena, sneakers on, breathing hard.

"Hey, April!"

She must have her headphones blasting because she doesn't even glance over. She jogs through the gravel parking lot and back around the other side of the arena.

I take a seat on a window ledge at the side of the building and pull out my crumpled MVP Super Training Plan from my backpack. *Go jogging once a week.* Ugh. Does April have her own secret training plan that I don't know about? I wiggle my toes in my flip-flops. I guess today is not the day I start jogging.

Crunch, crunch, crunch. A few moments later April is back on her next lap. How long has she been here?

I notice that she's running kind of funny, tugging on her pants every few strides. The elastic must be going in the waist or something. April usually sports the tightest designer athletic wear, but these pants look like they're about ready to fall off.

The gravel crunches again, louder this time, as Queenie's SUV pulls into the parking lot.

"Hey, jammer girl!" she yells. "You're early!"

"Hi, Queenie. Yeah, I wanted to get here and on skates as soon as possible so I could work on my footwork before we get started on practice."

"Wow! So motivated. Must be those pancakes giving you all the extra energy. All right, let's head in. Isn't that April's car?"

April jogs into view, and Queenie waves her down.

"Just getting in a bit of extra cross-training, Coach." April takes a swig from her water bottle. Is it just the way the sun is hitting her, or are those dark circles under her eyes?

Maybe I should tell April about my own cross-training plan and how getting enough sleep is high up on that list. Annie Mossity's blog says—

Then again, it's not like April invited me to jog with her. She doesn't want to help *me* get better, so why should I share my research with her? If April has her own secret jammer plan, I'll just keep mine to myself too. Fair is fair, right?

"I thought you wanted to work on that footwork!" Queenie calls to me from the arena door.

"Coming, Coach!"

Crunch, crunch, crunch. I look back and see that April has grabbed her gear and is on her way in too, hiking up her pants as she goes.

Chapter Eight

"All right, skaters, bring it in!"

Coach Queenie does a hockey stop with a screech in center track.

When Queenie calls for your attention, you had better give it to her. Quinoa Queen has been playing derby for years and coaching the "bigs" junior team (that's us, the over-twelves) for the last four. She has a way of making people listen. I thought she was maybe a teacher in her other life. Turns out, she's the head chef at some brunch place downtown. She's used to ordering people around.

"I'm not starting until everyone is in the center. Come on now, let's focus. If you can't gear up faster, you'll need to arrive earlier. Kat N. Crunch, I'm looking at you!"

"Sorry, Coach!" Kat yells and scrambles to pull on her elbow pads.

While the squad coasts in and forms a semicircle around Coach, April does crunches on the concrete floor. I can hear her counting under her breath. What is her plan? I need to figure it out, or I will have no chance of making MVP. Exercising anytime there's a break in practice? She must be really committed to upping her game too. Or she's just trying to make the rest of us look bad.

"Okay, now that everyone is here and paying attention—April, you too—I'll explain the drill," says Queenie. April sits up and stretches forward over her legs.

"As we learned from our last game, there is not just one kind of jamming in roller derby. Strength is just as important as agility, and the best jammers use a combination of both to help them get through a pack. Against a tough team that covers their lines like Uptown, sometimes you have to push a wall instead of trying to go around it. That's what we're going to work on today."

Queenie starts picking skaters to demonstrate the drill. Three of our best blockers set up a tough-looking three-wall on the straightaway. Any jammer would have to psych herself up speeding toward that wall. Well, maybe any jammer besides April.

Kat, covering the inside line, plays varsity rugby at school, and running into her is like hitting a brick wall. She presses her hip into Jackie Oh Dear, who is barely five feet tall but who is alarmingly quick on her feet. String Bean takes the outside. She's a gangly skater with surprising stability and long, long legs. They're a funny-looking combo—one short, one tall, but tough—I sure wouldn't want to face them in a game.

"The job of the jammer in this drill is not to dance around, but to push the blockers out of play." I sit up as straight as I can and try to catch Queenie's eye. I did this at the game! I pushed! *Come on, Queenie. Let me demo the drill for once!*

"April, can you come show us this skill?" Of course she picks April, as usual. Miss Gets-to-demo-every-single-drill *and* make it look easy.

April nods, pulls herself to her feet and rolls up behind the wall. I'd be shaking, having to face our best blockers in front of everyone, but April yawns and sets up between Kat and Jackie.

Screeee! On the whistle April tucks her shoulder and pushes, and pushes, and pushes. Nothing happens.

The wall digs in hard, holding themselves together and refusing to roll. April barely moves them a foot, let alone across the pivot line to end the drill. She backs off a few feet and tries again, this time between Jackie and Bean, but their brakes are on and her push gets her nowhere.

Queenie blows four whistles to end the drill. "Great wall. Let's try this again, shall we? Robin!"

Wait, me?

"Robin, want to give it a go? You were pushing Uptown all over the track."

My first demo drill! I jump to my feet so fast I almost fall backward. "Yes, Coach!"

The whole team is watching me. Everyone. But I *know* I can do this. I got enough sleep. I ate a snack. I turned up for practice early. My MVP Super Plan is in action!

Screee! I tuck my shoulder between Kat and Jackie and dig my toe-stops into the concrete, pressing into them with the whole side of my body. The wall starts to creep forward, and they push against me to stop my roll. Still, I'm gaining momentum. I can feel my teammates giving ground to my push, and we roll faster and faster. As we glide across the pivot line, Queenie whistles the drill over. She nods, and I *think* she maybe winks at me, but I can't be sure. All I know is that I'm trying to keep a check on the grin that wants to take over my face.

Did April see me kill that drill? Is she mad I did it better? I glance across the circle of skaters waiting for their turn to push a wall. April's not even in center track anymore. At the far side of the arena, earbuds in, April skates long, lone endurance laps, tugging up her pants every few strides. I can't believe it. She wasn't even watching.

Chapter Nine

"Okay, let's loosen up our hips with the pigeon stretch. Hold for thirty seconds..."

Kat leads the stretch, and we follow along, leaving dark, sweaty butt and leg prints all over the concrete floor. Postgame practices are always tough, but a steady stream of "good job" and "great push!" from Queenie got me through.

"Robin, you're sticking around for the littles practice, right? Amy could use the extra help," Queenie says as the team moves into a butterfly stretch. "I've got a meeting, and that's a lot of kids for Amy to coach on her own."

"You got it, Coach!" Getting to practice early is in my Super Plan, but staying after practice helps too. The more time on skates, the better. It doesn't hurt that coaching the littles is always a lot of fun. Those kids have this wide-eyed way of looking at you when you show them a new skill, even if it's just how to turn around or skate on one foot. It's hard not to feel like a superstar in front of cheering eight-year-olds.

"Great! Well, since you don't need to cool down quite yet, can you go grab the cooler in the referee room?" Queenie points across the arena. "I've got a treat for the team."

I sprint to the ref room, ignoring the dull ache of exhaustion in my legs.

A cooler can only mean one thing. My mouth waters as I flip open the lid. Popsicles! I snag a purple one (Of course! Team color!) and hold it in my mouth as I lug the cooler to center track.

Everyone digs in. April's earbuds must be blasting because she's still skating laps, forward, backward, clockwise, around the outside of the track. The popsicles are disappearing fast. She's going to miss out.

I grab the last purple one and sprint to catch her mid-lap. Usually she's so fast I wouldn't bother. It's easier to wait for her to finish a lap than try to keep up. But her pace is slower today.

"April, I saved you a popsicle."

She pops out her earbuds and skids to a stop. "Nah, I'm good. Give it to one of the littles, thanks." She puts the buds back in and returns to her laps, alternating sprints with sets of sit-ups and squats. April is clearly on some kind of plan, but after seeing how that pushing drill went, I'm not so sure it's working.

Chapter Ten

"Popsicles! Mum, look! They have popsicles!"

I watch Queenie and Amy's daughter drop her backpack and bolt for the cooler. I can't actually remember what her real name is. Everyone calls her Mean Sprout. Hurricane Amy follows a few paces behind, bending to collect the tiny elbow and knee-pads in Sprout's wake.

"Hi, Mom! Can I have a popsicle?" Sprout yells as she skids to center track. Queenie picks Sprout up and spins around on her skates. Sprout squeals and laughs.

"Of course. But don't make a mess." Queenie lowers Sprout down and points at Amy. "And go help Mum with your backpack first, young lady. You can't play derby if you don't have the right gear. And you can't go dropping it all over the place and expect other people to pick it up for you!"

Sprout skips back over to Amy. "Sorry, Mum." She scoops up her bag in both arms and waddles toward the cooler. Amy, a few steps behind, collects the wristguards and mouthguard that spill out. "*Now* can I have a popsicle?"

"Yes, Sprout," Queenie and Amy answer in unison.

"All right, I'm off to my meeting. Thanks for helping out, Robin!" Queenie heads for the change room. "Have a good practice!"

The other littles trickle into the arena one by one, hugging their parents at the door. "See you in an hour, kiddo!"

"Coach Robin is going to hand out some treats while I set up the practice cones!" Amy hollers from across the track.

A dozen littles wobble and trip toward center track on their tiny skates. They line up, and I hand them each a popsicle while checking over their gear. "An orange one for you! Nope, that elbow pad is upside down! Here's a green one. Wait, that wrist-guard goes on your right hand! The other right hand! That's the one!"

Some of the youngest, like Sprout, have orange or blue popsicle juice smeared all over their faces.

"Oops, Mum, I made a mess!" Sprout laughs as Amy returns to center track.

"You definitely did, Sprout, and you're not the only one!" Amy eyes the sticky hands and faces around her. "Robin, would you mind grabbing some napkins for us, so the pack doesn't get stuck together?"

I go grab a bundle from the bathroom dispenser and coast back to the track. I've only been gone a minute, but the littles are already sitting story-time style in a circle around Amy. I try my best to pass napkins to the messiest littles without disrupting Amy's first drill.

"So it's not going to make me fat?" One of the littles holds out her unopened popsicle. "I don't have to only eat salad? My sister said—"

"No way, Pumpkin! There's nothing wrong with a treat now and again if we eat healthy most of the time and stay active," Amy says with a smile. "Don't you think so, Robin?"

"I know so!" I answer. I can't believe an eight-year-old is worried about getting fat! What would Annie Mossity say? "Your body needs food to do all the amazing things it does and keep you active. And what's our favorite way to stay active?"

A chorus of voices calls out, "Roller derby!"

Pumpkin smiles and unwraps her blue popsicle.

I watch the littles wobble across the rink, practicing their one-foot skating. Eight-year-olds counting calories? I can't believe it.

"Look, Robin, I'm doing it! I'm doing it!" Pumpkin shrieks as she rolls cone to cone on one foot.

"That's awesome, Pumpkin! It must be that popsicle! Keep it up!" I holler back at her. Pumpkin grins, switches feet, stumbles and falls. "You okay?"

The little girl springs back up with a smile, dusts herself off, ready to try again. "Yeah, I'm okay, Robin! I've got popsicle power!"

Chapter Eleven

"Thanks again for all your help today, Robin!" Amy shouts as I head for the change room to finally gear down.

"No problem!" And it really isn't. Coaching the littles doesn't even feel like work because they're just so positive. *Here, jump this cone. Okay, Coach Robin! Okay, now turn around like this! Okay, Coach Robin!* They want to try everything, and they don't mind if they fall. They're just happy to get back up and try again.

"But really, if you want to talk about anything at all—"

Yikes, what did I walk into? A stone-faced Queenie is sitting across from April. I didn't even know April was still here. And didn't Queenie have to leave for a meeting?

"Really, I think I just had the flu or something. I've been working really hard at school, pre-law applications, exams, all that stuff. It wears you down..."

Queenie must be concerned after all about April's sudden drop in performance. Maybe she's taking her off the jammer rotation?

"Stress is one thing, April, but—"

The door, held open by my one skate, squeaks, and Queenie and April turn to face me.

"Sorry, sorry! I didn't realize anyone was in here."

I duck out before they respond and decide to de-gear on the bench with the littles. Amy is still trying to wipe the last smudges of popsicle off their faces while they wait for their parents to arrive.

I've heard the twelfth graders talking about all the applications they have to do for schools. If April's trying to get into pre-law, she's working even harder. I can't imagine trying to keep straight As *and* play derby at the same time. But somehow perfect April has always done it. I guess she's just starting to crack.

"All right, famjam," hollers Queenie, pushing open the change-room door and switching back to Mom mode, "meeting's over! Let's go get some eats!"

"Yay, Mum! Mom can come to dinner after all!" Mean Sprout starts shoving her gear into her backpack. A kneepad sneaks out and clatters onto the floor. "Robin says I have to eat for fuel! I vote mac and cheese!"

I've got my gear packed up, and Amy's ready to lock the arena doors, but there's no sign of April.

"Should I go check on her, Coach?" I don't know if I want to go in there.

Before Queenie can reply, the change-room door squeaks open and April emerges, lugging her gear. She's thrown on her league hoodie, and it looks like it's swallowing her whole. She struggles under the weight of her backpack.

"What have you got in there, bricks?" Amy jokes, trying to press April into a smile.

"Something like that," April mutters without looking up. She stalks out the door and into the parking lot.

"You good for a ride, Robin?" Queenie asks.

"Yep, that's my mom pulling in now."

"Okay, thanks again for your help. See you next week!"

I open the car door and inhale a delicious cloud. My mom has ordered takeout. Mmmmmm, pad thai! Just what I need after a long practice.

"Hey, Superstar!" I pick up the steaming container on the passenger seat and sit down. "Who's the new girl?" she asks.

New girl? Who is she talking about? I look across the parking lot and see

Queenie, Amy and Sprout climbing into their car.

"You mean Queenie and Amy's kid? They had her like, forever ago. She's eight!" I laugh. My mom totally has the worst memory.

"No, silly! The skinny girl in the big black hoodie," my mom answers. "She came out just before you. I've never seen her before."

My mom turns the key in the ignition and starts the car.

"Mom," I say. "That skinny girl was April."

Chapter Twelve

Come on, computer, let's go! Fueled by spicy noodles and the contagious excitement of the littles, I'm tapping my foot against my chair, willing the web page to load.

In the time it took for my computer to actually move past the start screen, I polished off the last spring roll. The home page finally flickers onto the screen. I toss my takeout container into the trash.

Where is that Annie Mossity blog about nutrition and stuff? I know I've pinned it before, but I can't seem to dig it up. I want to print out copies for the littles. Maybe

Pumpkin will stop listening to that crap about watching her calories. Who cares what her sister says? The real question is, what would Annie Mossity do?

Healthy eating, sports. Search.

Look at all these weird diets. Every other article suggests a different one. Eat grapefruit, drink juice, go low-carb. What about just eating healthy foods, like vegetables and stuff? Annie Mossity's blog is buried in here somewhere.

Healthy eating, roller derby. Search.

Here it is! *"The Importance of Fueling Your Body for Your Tough-as-Hell Sport."* That's more like it. *Getting enough of the right kind of fuel can make or break you as an athlete. Roller derby is a tough sport that requires lots of muscle power and endurance. Eating too little food, or the wrong foods, won't give your muscles the fuel they need to get you through a practice, let alone a game.*

Save. Print. Who could argue with one of the best skaters in the country?

I see that Annie's blog has a lot more cool articles. "*Annie Mossity's 'Drop It Like a Squat' Workout.*" Pin it!

"*Explosive Power for Pushy Jammers.*" Pin that too!

Is this what they call a "pin hole"? Blog post after cool blog post fills up my pin board. I collect hours of reading for later. "*Roller Derby Burpee Challenge.*" Pin it! That can definitely help with my MVP Super Plan.

What's this one? A core workout? "*Suggested Pins in Health and Wellness*" brings up a photo of six-pack abs with no workout link in sight. The caption at the bottom reads, *You have to make a choice: abs or pasta*. Who cares what my abs look like as long as they keep me standing and skating, right?

The more I pin workout routines and healthy eating, the more of this kind of six-pack "inspiration" pops up in my suggestions. Sleek, thin, bikini-clad bodies, with *skinny feels better than cake tastes* pasted over in giant text. *Sweat is fat crying*, the captions say. *The hunger means it's working.*

Yikes! As if being thin is all that matters in sports. I'm certainly not six-pack thin, and I think I'm pretty fit. I'm a derby girl, aren't I?

I click back to my own derby pin page and scroll past photos of my favorite skaters. Annie Mossity, of course, muscular and tough but not "thin" like those images. Her teammates, some of the top-ranked skaters in the world, range in body type: big, small, wiry, stocky and everything in between.

My favorite photo of Annie shows her in jammer-line stance, glaring at the camera with this slight smirk on her face. I think I've pinned it five times, and I don't care. She looks so strong and confident. Like she's ready to leap off the jam line and blast through those blockers, no problem. *That's* what I want to look like.

This photo was also pinned to the board Roller Derby by A. Powers.

A. Powers. April Powers. I didn't even know she was on here! Maybe I can steal some of her cross-training ideas and work them into my Super Plan. I don't follow her board, but maybe she pinned them publicly. Let's find out. Click.

April's derby board is surprisingly small, a Christmas-stocking pattern of a roller skate instead of a sock, a couple of stills from some old derby movie where no one is wearing helmets, the awesome photo of Annie and some *really* expensive skates she's probably drooling over for a graduation present.

It looks like she has a separate Workout board. This must be where she's hiding her jammer secrets. If I nab April's workout plan, maybe I can steal MVP too.

April is definitely not trying to learn how to do a better push-up or how to run longer without hurting her knees. Her so-called Workout board is full of all that "never too thin" crap. April has even added little captions of her own: *Gotta stay in control*, and *Don't let the hunger get you down*, and *It's all going to be worth it*.

Holy crap. There is something seriously up with April. No wonder she's losing all her power. She's practically vanishing into her baggy clothes, and she's doing it all on purpose. By next week who knows how much of April will even be left?

I've got to tell Queenie. She'll know what to do. She's a chef—she understands healthy eating, right? But April will frigging kill me if she finds out I told. She doesn't know I've seen her board, and she already barely talks to me. If I rat her out, she's going to be furious.

Maybe I can wait and see. I mean, she's still coming to practice. Queenie has to notice eventually, right? Before her plan gets dangerous? Plus, if April wants to lose weight, who am I to tell her not to? I mean, all it's doing so far is making her worse at derby.

If she keeps this up, the MVP trophy April didn't even want will be her last. Maybe it will be my turn to start picking up hardware every game.

With April slowly disappearing, this might be my only chance to be the jammer star. It couldn't hurt to wait and see, right?

Chapter Thirteen

What would Annie Mossity do?

I couldn't get Annie's photo out of my head last night. Would Annie let her teammate put herself in danger, just for an MVP award? *You're right, Annie. No way.*

But April's still going to kill me if I tell on her. Maybe she's not even the same A. Powers I found online. Before I talk to Queenie, I need to make sure that April is *really* in trouble.

Mom's happy to drop me off at practice a half hour early again. I told her jammers have to get there early to practice together. Sure enough, April's car is in the lot, and she is lacing up her sneakers to run her pre-practice laps.

"Hey, April! How's it going? You're here early again, eh?" I try to make casual conversation. "My mom had to get to work, but she left a snack for me. Want some of my apple slices and peanut butter?"

Step one: offer April food and see what happens.

April glances up and shakes her head. "No, thanks. Eating before exercise makes me sick to my stomach." From the look of her, she's already sick to her stomach. Her cheeks look gray. Maybe it's just the sun reflecting off the gravel.

"Oh, okay. Hey, so you did such a great job with that apex jump and everything in the last game, I was hoping you could give me some jammer advice. There's no littles practice today, so we could grab a bite after our practice and chat. I can get my mom to pick me up later. My treat!"

"Sorry, Robin. I...I have plans. I have an appointment to get my dress altered. Prom is in a couple weeks, and I need it taken in."

Her prom dress doesn't fit her anymore? I guess that's not surprising.

"Oh yeah, I totally forgot it was almost prom, being a junior and everything. I'm not going, because *as if* any senior would ask me. I'm not super into dressing up anyway. Who are you going with?"

April purses her lips. "No one. I mean, no one yet. There's this guy who is going to...who is supposed to ask me. He plays lacrosse. He just hasn't...yet."

"Oh, well, I'm sure he will. You're so cool and smart and stuff." *Stop gushing, Robin.* "Well, I'm going to eat my snack now—fuel up. You sure you don't want any?"

"Nah, but you can wait in my car if you want." It had started spitting rain. "You don't want your gear getting wet." April finishes tying her shoe, pops her earbuds in and takes off around the building.

She definitely isn't biting on the food. But is that really enough evidence to tattle to Queenie?

Sitting in the passenger seat of April's car and crunching apple slices, I hear a blip from the console. April has left her phone charging in the car. The pin app lights up the screen. *New pins suggested for you in "fitness."* I can't help it. I have to open the app and see what she's been pinning.

A stock image of some bony model in a ball gown with words pasted over top: *How to lose 20 pounds in two weeks.*

A. Powers has captioned the photo: *ten down, ten to go.*

April's secret plan has nothing to do with becoming a better jammer. She wants to lose twenty pounds, and she's already halfway there.

If she keeps this up, she's going to disappear altogether.

I have to tell Queenie.

Chapter Fourteen

Queenie crunches into the parking lot. April is out of sight on the other side of the arena. Great timing! I can talk to Queenie right now, and April will never know. I jump out of April's car and jog over to Queenie's. I tap on the window.

"Whoa, whoa, whoa, jammer girl. What's the big hurry? And why were you in April's car?"

My words came out all together. "I got dropped off early and it was raining but I really have to talk to you about something okay?"

"Whoa. Slow it down a notch, kiddo. Grab these cones and help me bring them into the arena. Then we'll talk, okay?"

With a stack of cones almost as tall as me in my arms, I follow Queenie into the arena. "Listen, I know you wanted to chat, but how about we make it after practice? I've got a big announcement to prepare for the team. I want to make sure I have all the details set up, okay?"

April, her hair wet and stringy from the rain, strides into the arena with her gear bag over one shoulder and her phone in hand. Her phone. Did I relock the screen after I snooped? April doesn't look my way, so I think I'm in the clear. *Phew*.

There's no point in trying to talk to Queenie with April in earshot anyway. I'll have to wait until she leaves.

"Okay, Coach. Sounds good." I drop the cones in the center of the track. What's this big announcement though? A new transfer skater? It had better not be someone else who is going to push me out of the running for that MVP spot.

After the rest of the team rolls in and skates a few warm-up laps, Queenie whistles and calls us into the center of the track with her usual stern practice voice. "Bring it in!"

April, earbuds in, is doing her usual laps and sit-ups circuit.

"That means you, too, Powers!"

April screeches to a halt and coasts toward the rest of the team.

When she has all our eyes, Coach begins. "You all know that we have our big season closer game coming up in a couple weeks. And that it's against one of the toughest teams in the area, Midtown Mini Mayhem."

Kat scowls. "They're good. But we're good. We're better!"

"I have every faith that you can totally win it!" continues Queenie. "However, what I wanted to add is that we will have a guest joining us in the audience for the game."

Oh, thank god. Not a guest skater. Just an audience guest. Maybe it's the mayor or a sponsor or something. The owner of the Pancake Hut?

"I'm sure you're all familiar with Creek City's adult team, the one Amy and I play on. Well, one of our teammates will be sitting in the audience, doing a little scouting for next season."

An A-team scout? Usually you have to wait until after you've turned eighteen to try out for the adult-level teams. Which can mean waiting a whole year depending on when your birthday falls. A scout coming to invite the best seventeen-year-olds to step up when they age out is a huge deal. Damn, why do I have to still be sixteen?

"Which skater is coming to watch, Queenie?" Suddenly April is *very* interested in listening to what Queenie has to say. She's almost eighteen, and this could be her big opportunity. I might be imagining it, but it seems like her voice wavered a little as she asked.

"Annie Mossity."

The team erupts in nervous chatter. *The* Annie Mossity. One of the top skaters ever, anywhere. *The* Annie Mossity who dominates my pin board. My derby idol and

81

everyone else's, by the look of it. I might just have a heart attack. Annie Mossity is coming to watch me play. In two weeks. I need to step up my game. I can't let Annie down.

As scary as this is for me, it's got to be scarier for April. One game can now make her derby career and move her up to the adult league. In less than a month, she could be Annie's teammate.

This has got to snap April out of her obsession with being thin. Maybe I won't have to tell Queenie after all. I haven't even met Annie Mossitiy and somehow my hero is still saving my day.

Chapter Fifteen

"Grab your black and white shirts, team— we're scrimmaging!"

Ah, scrimmage practice. No drills, no skating laps, just a full hour of jams against your own teammates. There's no crowd to cheer us on, but I still get the nervous flutters when I step out to jam.

One, two, one, two, one, two... Queenie numbers us and splits us up evenly. Of course, April is jamming for the opposite team.

Every time I step off the jammer line, I keep my feet away from the edges of the track and push as hard as I can. First up jamming against me is Kat, who puts all her weight against my team's wall, driving them forward way faster than I can. I'm not lead, but I'm out of the pack, and I zip up behind Kat, forcing her to call off the jam with no points for either of us. Zero-zero is better than a loss anyway. Cool, calm and safe jamming is *my* style.

Next up, April slips through a hole on the inside line and skips out of the pack untouched. Classic frigging April. On her second pass the wall is ready, and they swallow her up. No amount of pushing and dancing around will open up the wall for her. With Jackie Oh Dear approaching fast behind her, she calls the jam off to save the points. Another zero-zero. April hangs her head as she rolls to the bench.

When April and I finally face off on the jammer line, she shifts back and forth behind me, trying to confuse my blockers.

"Don't dance with her—just hold her once she chooses a spot," Queenie shouts from the bench. "Robin, get ready to make that strong hit off the whistle! Powers, keep it simple!"

Screeeee!

April pauses off the line and doesn't move forward. I burst into the pack and make two quick hits to open up a lane. With one blocker to beat, I press my shoulder against her chest and push until the referee calls her out of play. She lets me go. Two whistles blast, and I'm lead against April Powers.

I turn back to the pack as I drop into my crossover stance and skate my solitary lap. My blockers call out April's moves—"Inside line! Outside line!"—and I hear them knock her down over and over, kneepads clattering on the ground. Her team swings into action, hitting my blockers, but they can't keep them away from April.

We practice like we play. It's no good to baby your friends. Zooming toward the pack, I realize that April's team doesn't even see me coming. They're too busy trying to clear a lane for her to escape. This is my turn to make it through untouched!

I take a chance and skate the wide-open outside line, dodging the last blocker. She sees me too late to make any contact.

"That's it, Robin, keep skating. Don't call it off. April, look for your pivot. Pass the star if you're stuck!"

The star pass. Another move April Powers has never found herself forced to make. If she can get the jammer cover to her pivot, April can switch to blocking and send her pivot out to jam.

"I got this, Coach!" April gasps as String Bean lays a hit on her that takes out her legs again. April's face is growing red, and she's struggling to pull herself up off the floor.

Every time she gets up, boom, another hit takes her down. I spot an open gap between blockers and sneak right down the middle of the track. The whole team is frazzled, trying to set April free.

I'm on my way out of the pack again when I hear four sharp whistles.

I didn't call it off. I was kicking butt on that jam. There's no way that was two whole minutes. *What the heck, Queenie?*

"Take a knee, take a knee!" Queenie sprints to the pack, where a circle has formed around someone on the ground.

"Someone call 9-1-1!" Kat yells. "It's April. She collapsed!"

Chapter Sixteen

"Let us know how everything goes!" Queenie taps the side of April's dad's car before it pulls out of the parking lot.

April is pale but conscious in the passenger seat.

"Okay, skaters, let's call that a practice. Everyone go grab your stuff. Gear down." Queenie collects April's gear from the track. There had been no ambulance, no sirens or anything cool like that. Just April coming to, and Queenie putting a cool cloth on her head while she waited for her dad to turn up.

Back in the arena, the team prods Queenie for details. "Is she going to be okay?" "Can I go with her?" "What happened?" "Is she sick?"

"April's heading to the hospital with her dad. She'll let us know when she's feeling better. For now, let's all make time for a good stretch before we head home. You don't want to be too sore for next practice."

"Ummmm...Coach Queenie..." I tap Queenie on the shoulder as she lugs April's gear bag to the referee room.

"What's up, jammer girl?"

"Ummmm... I don't know how to say this. Or if it's anything. But I think I might know what's been going on with April."

My teammates stretch their legs at the far end of the arena. I follow Queenie into the referee room, and we sit on the benches that line the walls.

"Go on, Robin."

"Well, I go on this site where people share and pin all the stuff they are interested in and inspired by and stuff like that—"

"Yes, Robin, I know the site you mean. I use it for recipes, and crafts for Sprout. What about it?"

"Well, I accidentally found April's pin board on there. And I thought it would be cool derby stuff. But it wasn't. It was kind of weird—stuff about being fat, and losing weight fast."

Queenie sighs. "And you're sure it was her? She was pinning about unhealthy weight loss?"

"Yeah, I mean, please don't tell her I told you or anything, but she posted about losing twenty pounds before prom. Stuff like *hunger is fat crying*, and how she's got ten pounds left to go."

Queenie undoes her helmet and pulls it off her head. She combs her hand through her damp hair. "This is pretty serious, you know that, right, Robin? If what you're telling me is true, April might be in real trouble."

"Is she going to be able to play the season closer? With Annie Mossity watching?"

"I don't know, Robin. This is a lot more serious than a roller-derby game. I'm going to give April's dad a call tonight and chat with him. Thank you for telling me."

So April might be out for the big game, which leaves the MVP spot open for me. But that lump rises up in my throat again. Sure, I could snag the MVP trophy, but will it feel the same if April's not skating? If she's stuck in the hospital?

Chapter Seventeen

"All right, team, grab some water and bring it in!" A dozen sets of skates screech to a halt in center track as we circle around Queenie.

Suddenly I'm soaked. *Great.* The lid of my water bottle clatters onto the concrete as I dump the whole thing down my shirt. *A perfect start to my practice.*

"Not quite time to hit the showers yet, Robin, but I can't fault your enthusiasm," Queenie jokes. "So, the big game is next Saturday, and if we're going to win, we're really going to have to pull ourselves together as a team."

"What are we going to do without April?" Jackie blurts. "I mean, she's our best jammer. No offense, Robin."

Ouch. Thanks, Jackie. But maybe she's right. We do need April. Super MVP Plan or not, I'm just not as strong as she is.

"We are a team, not just one skater. Sometimes injuries happen, and we will have to play this game together. No matter what our original plan is. I believe in us!"

"But Queenie, who's—"

Creaaaaak. The hinges on the back arena door squeak as it opens, letting a splash of sun into the dark hallway.

Our team breaks into hushed chatter. "Is that her?" "Is she back?" "Has she said anything to you?" "She hasn't even been online."

April, gear bag noticeably absent from her back, baseball cap low and sunglasses hiding her face, walks into the arena and into the first change room.

A grin slides over Jackie's face. "April's back!"

April's back? Already? There goes my chance at MVP. She's going to get back on the track and effortlessly glide through the blockers just like she always does. My stomach turns over. Shouldn't I be happy that my teammate is alive and not eating mush in a hospital somewhere?

"So is she going to skate? We're going to kick Midtown's butt now that April's back!" Kat is on her feet, suddenly ready to skate all the laps Queenie demands.

"April has offered to come help us out tonight, but she hasn't been cleared for contact yet. We'll be working on fast laps and crossovers, and April will be timing us and helping correct our form."

"What do you mean *cleared for contact?*"

"Is she sick? Is she hurt?"

"I heard she hasn't even been back to school yet."

"What about Annie Mossity and the game?"

"I wonder if she's still going to prom."

My stomach does another flip. No derby. No school. No scout. And all because I ratted her out.

April must be so mad at me.

Chapter Eighteen

"Kat, 14.5. Gotta speed that up. Jackie, 11.8. Good—way to go. Robin, 10.9. Roxy, 12.2—almost there."

Ball cap and sunglasses still on, like a celebrity ducking the paparazzi, April stands center track, stopwatch around her neck, clicking its stop/start button. She calls out our lap times in a bored voice and tacks on hints here and there. I have the lowest time by far, but April doesn't even comment.

"Ali, 13.9—that's it. Better. Crasher, 11.7—bend those knees. Robin, 10.5."

I've got to say something to her. I skate over to April while other skaters take their turns. I breathe in hard and tap her on the shoulder. She doesn't turn around. April doesn't look any thinner than when I saw her carted off to the hospital, but I'm not sure she looks any healthier either. She's wearing her giant team hoodie and loose sweats. She still looks like she might vanish into them.

"Umm...April..."

"15.2. Keep trying out there. Bend your knees."

"April..."

"11.4. That's a lot better. Good job."

"April..."

"*What*, Robin?" April spins around to face me. Even though she still has her glasses on, I feel like she's shooting laser beams right through me.

"Um, April, I wanted to, ummm...see how you're doing?"

"How am I doing? How do you think I'm doing, Robin?" April hisses.

Queenie blows a long, sweeping whistle to call the skaters to the far end of the track.

"You're back at practice, so that's good, right? I hope you're feeling better and stuff..."

Queenie blows her whistle again to call us over. "Let's go, team! We've got work to do!"

I turn to skate toward the group, but April grabs my arm. "I know it was you," she mutters under her breath. "Who ratted me out. You snooped on my phone. I know you did it because you want me to fail."

"April. I..." I can't deny it. I *did* tell on her. But I thought I was helping.

"No, don't *April, I...* me with this fake-innocent, trying-your-best attitude. What, you were trying to help? Trying to help me get stuck in hospital for a week? Trying to help me have to skip a week of school when I have pre-law applications to finish and top marks to earn in all my classes? Trying to help me fail my exams and *not* get asked to prom?"

"April, I was worried about you. I wouldn't have said anything unless...you seemed really sick..."

"You have no fricking idea, Robin. No idea what is going on in my life or the pressure I'm under. All you do in your free time is gush over celebrity skaters and creep me online."

April lifts her glasses, wipes her eyes and then rearranges the frames on her face. The light catches the dark circles under her eyes.

"April, I didn't mean to hurt your feelings. I just wanted to help you."

"Well, stop trying to help me. Mind your own damn business, Robin. I've already got my parents looking over my shoulder every five minutes and forcing all sorts of food on me. I don't need your so-called help too. Get out of my life. And get real while you're at it. With or without me on the track, you're never going to be MVP."

She throws the stopwatch onto the ground and then stomps away toward the change room.

The lump starts rising in my throat. I blink my eyes to press it back down. *No crying in derby. No crying in derby.*

"Robin, are you part of this team? Because we're down here practicing while you're gabbing!" Queenie hollers from the end of the gym.

"Coming!" I wipe my eyes with the back of my wristguard. April isn't doing any better, and there's no way they're going to let her play that game if she keeps shrinking away. But she told me to get out of her life. Maybe she deserves to not get scouted if she can't accept help from people who care about her.

It would be easy to just let April disappear. Getting MVP would be a piece of cake if she wasn't there to stop me. But I need her on skates and playing to prove that I *can* beat her.

Plus, no matter how mean she is, April's in some serious trouble. And it doesn't look like anyone is getting through to her, not her parents, not even Queenie and definitely not me.

I have an idea. Maybe there is one person who might be able to help.

Chapter Nineteen

It's been four whole days and still no answer.

I've been racing home every day after school, booting up the old computer, drumming my fingers on the desk and waiting for what seems like hours for my email to load. Four days in a row, and all I've got to show for it are pin-board suggestions and ads for sales on jeans.

I had re-read my message probably sixteen times before I finally hit the Send button on the contact form. Still, maybe I shouldn't have bothered. Maybe Annie thought I sounded like a tattletale. Or just another fan reaching out through her website. Superstar jammers are busy. They probably don't have the time to read every email they get.

"See you later, Mom!" I slam the car door and crunch across the gravel toward the arena. For the first time since I was a fresh skater, I don't even want to be at practice. What if Annie finally messages me back?

Who am I kidding? Why would an email from some no-name junior matter to one of the best skaters in the whole country?

"Get in there and gear up, jammer girl." Queenie surprises me just inside the arena doors. "Amy's on her way too." We've got a special practice lined up today. The littles are going to be here to work with us."

What could the littles team possibly be doing with us? We can't hit them. I mean, they can barely hit each other. We have a huge game coming up, and Queenie wants us to practice with the littles? Isn't that a waste of time?

The arena door swings open, and April wanders in, her gear bag slung over her shoulder for the first time since her collapse. That's a good sign for the game at least. And I can't beat her for MVP if she isn't skating. She's carrying a bottle of something thick and sludgy.

"Welcome back, Powers!" Queenie yells at her from center track, where she's going over her practice notes. "Shake first, then get that gear on. Practice starts in fifteen minutes."

"Yes, Coach." April scowls and tips some of the green sludge toward her mouth. "Ugh." She sits on the bench and begins putting on her pads, pulling faces and taking sips of her shake.

Hurricane Amy strolls into the arena, holding Mean Sprout by the hand. "Is she really coming to see us? Hey, hey, Mum, is she really?" Mean Sprout skips across the arena toward me. "Robin! Robin! Guess what? Mom and Mum say—"

"That's enough, Sprout." Amy cuts her off. "Don't ruin the surprise."

By the time Kat, Jackie and the rest of the bigs roll into the arena, there are ten or eleven littles running around the place.

"What are they doing here? I didn't think they even had practice today," Kat whispers to Jackie.

"Queenie said we're doing practice together, but it doesn't look like they're skating. No gear," Jackie points out.

Before anyone can speculate further, Queenie blows a sweeping whistle. "Bring it in, everyone!"

"That means you too, littles!" Amy yells at a group of them playing leapfrog off to one side of the arena.

"Don't we have a game we have to practice for? What's going on, Coach?" April is geared up but still working on her shake. She crosses her arms and scoffs, "Do we really need the littles here tonight?"

Queenie addresses the whole group. "Take a seat on the floor, skaters, because tonight we have a special guest joining us."

"I know who it is! I know who it—"

"Hush, Sprout." Amy presses her finger to her lips.

"So who are we waiting on?" Just as April finishes her question, the arena door squeaks open, and a figure appears in the burst of light that floods in.

"Is that...?"

"Oh my god, it's her!"

"Skaters, I'd like you to welcome to our practice the one and only Annie Mossity."

Chapter Twenty

"Holy crap." April almost spits out her shake.

Whispers and giggles sweep through the arena.

"I told you I knew! I told you!" Sprout is on her feet, jumping up and down. Her light-up sneakers flash red and pink.

"Annie asked if she could come to our practice to talk to our junior skaters about an issue that is very important to her and to athletes in general." Queenie waves Annie toward the center of the track. "I'll let her tell you about it. Annie, take it away!"

Annie Mossity. *The* Annie Mossity! She's somehow even taller in person and looks so strong! She's wearing her purple All-Stars jersey, and her skates have matching purple toe caps. She floats to the center of the track, so effortlessly and easily on her skates. But so tough at the same time! I would *not* want her jamming toward me on a track. She looks like she could do some serious damage with those strong shoulders and hips.

"Thanks so much for having me at your practice, skaters!" The wristguard-plastic applause dies down.

"Who's that?" one of the littles whispers loudly to Sprout.

"Shhhh! She's famous!" Sprout squeaks back.

"Let me answer that question! For those who don't know, I'm Annie Mossity. I play for the Creek City All-Star team. I also do some private coaching and have a roller-derby blog where I share my thoughts on the sport. And a few drills here and there."

Across the circle of skaters surrounding Annie, April is staring. I half expect her to pull out a pen and start jotting down notes. I guess Annie is her hero too. Maybe we have something in common after all.

"I asked your coaches, the amazing Quinoa Queen and Hurricane Amy, if I could stop by your practice today to talk to you about nutrition and how important it is to roller derby or any other sport."

She must have read my message. It can't be a coincidence.

"As an athlete, and you are all roller-derby athletes, you need to remember that our bodies will only treat us as well as we treat them," she continues. "That means putting healthy foods in our bodies if we expect them to skate and jump and hit and spin as much as we ask them to."

We are all nodding. She has our undivided attention.

"Now, that may seem like an easy concept to understand, but things can be a lot more complicated than that. Maybe it hasn't happened yet for you little ones, but as you get older, there are a lot of pressures put on young women."

April is nodding along with the rest of us, perhaps without realizing it.

"There are a lot of ideas in the media, in magazines, online, pictures of what 'good' and 'bad' bodies look like. And there's a lot of push to try to look a certain way, to be thin enough to meet this silly standard."

April sniffles. Is she welling up?

"You may not believe this, but when I started really getting into roller derby, I had a lot of trouble accepting my own body. As I trained, I got stronger and in many ways bigger. I started taking up more space. But everywhere I looked there were images telling me to be smaller and thinner. Sure, my gameplay was improving every day. I knew I was way more fit than I had ever been, but I was so worried about fitting in. I worried that I was ugly or not pretty enough."

April pretends to be scratching her nose. But I see her flick a tear away.

"It took talking to my teammates, to my coaches, to my mom and my sisters, to my friends, to realize that I was being held back by these silly standards. That I needed to eat enough of the right foods to be a strong and healthy skater, to be a better athlete. And that my body was awesome and beautiful. It does so many cool things. It plays this totally cool sport! And so does yours. So now, whenever I go to a practice, or to a game, or for a jog or anything, I say thanks to my body for doing the amazing things it does for me, and for being strong and beautiful. I also show my thanks by making sure I feed it enough and feed it right."

Tears are rolling down April's cheeks. She's not even trying to hide them anymore.

Chapter Twenty-One

Annie sits in the front row at turn two, notebook and pen in hand. She's wearing her Creek City All-Stars track jacket, and two littles have already run over to snag her autograph for their bout programs. Ever since her chat with the league, the littles have been playing at being Annie Mossity all practice long. When they practice cone jumping, they high-five each other for being just like Annie jumping the apex.

Don't stare, Robin. Don't stare. After Annie's talk, I didn't have the guts to introduce myself to her. Plus, I had sent my message anonymously, so she wouldn't have known it was from me anyway. I still can't believe she showed up.

I wonder if April has seen Annie in the audience yet. She must have. April is quiet at the end of the bench, eyes closed, earbuds in her ears and a jammer cover on her helmet, waiting for the game to start. After three practices back on skates and what seemed like a lot of gross protein shakes, April is on the roster for the big game, and it looks like she's up first to jam.

I don't know what Annie said to April after making the speech to the league, but I saw them chatting at the end of the arena while the rest of us practiced the apex-jump move. Whatever it was must have made an impact, because ever since then April's been complaining less about choking back her shakes and has been working hard at practice. I even saw her take a couple of apple slices from Kat as they geared down after last practice.

"You ready to do this, team?" Coach Queenie has her own clipboard. We're all curious to know who is blocking together, who is jamming and who we are going to rely on when we get into a tough spot.

Queenie hands me the second jammer cover.

"You're up second, jammer girl. Show me what you got, okay?"

Immediately my stomach does a somersault. That orange wall on the track looks unbeatable. Even during the warm-up with their own jammers, they hit hard. That Midtown Mayhem wall is going to be mine to face. And Annie Mossity will be watching every jam. April's jams and mine.

The sweeping whistle starts the game, cutting into my panic. April lines up behind the jammer line and both sets of blockers.

"Welcome to the season-closer bout, featuring your very own Creek City Junior Roller Derby versus the Midtown Mini Mayhem!"

Jim the Announcer Guy spots April out on the jammer line.

"*And it looks like Creek City is playing its top-scoring jammer for this first jam. It's April Powers out on the jam line!*"

The crowd breaks into a cheer for April.

"*Now as we wait for the jam-start whistle, I guess it's fair to note that April has been out on an injury these last couple of weeks. But I guess she's been looking strong enough back at practice to start off this game for her team. Coach Quinoa Queen knows what she's doing, and she wouldn't field a jammer she doesn't trust in a game as important as this one—*"

"Five seconds!" The jam timer's yell echoes through the arena.

Scree!

"*And they're off! April Powers waits a beat before making her move into the outside of the pack—*"

There's the tiniest hole on the outside line of the orange wall, and our blockers have got their jammer tied up. April's been off skates for weeks. I don't know if she'll even try that dangerous of a move...

"*April Powers makes a daring move to the outside. Oh, it looks like that hole is about to close up—*"

In the audience, Annie's head is down, jotting notes in her book. She looks up just as April jumps up on her toe-stops and spins toward the hole on the outside line.

"*Oooooh! She's being forced to the outside line, on one foot. April Powers is inches away from a track-cut penalty here and—*"

Scree!

One whistle blast. A penalty.

Did April cut the track on the first jam? With Annie Mossity watching her every move, April Powers just might be headed to the penalty box.

Chapter Twenty-Two

"Orange, five-three, forearm!"

A roar rumbles through the crowd. April made it through the pack. On one foot. On *two wheels* of one foot.

Out in the audience, Annie is nodding and making marks in her notebook.

April, out of the pack, is making her way back on her scoring pass as lead jammer.

"Go, April, you've got ten feet!"

Only ten feet? Our team must have been caught up watching April spin and dance. The orange jammer has beat our blockers and is catching up fast. Judging by the way that other jammer is gaining, April may have her footwork back, but her power hasn't quite returned.

April looks behind her as she approaches the pack. She glides down the inside line around one orange blocker while tapping her hips to end the jam.

Her jam referee holds up one finger: 1-0. Not April's usual multipoint jam, but we're still winning. It hits me harder than Kat did in warm-up that it's now my turn to show Queenie and Annie what I can do.

"All right, jammer girl, you're on!" Queenie taps the star on the side of my helmet as I roll toward the jam line, avoiding tripping on the tape this time.

The other jammer is a short girl with her hair in a ponytail that goes down her back, so I can't read her name.

"*Robin CookieJars from Creek City is on the jam line. Robin helped bring Creek City back from a big deficit last game here against Uptown. Let's see if she can put some points on the scoreboard in this jam!*"

Gulp. Jim the Announcer Guy thinks I'm going to score points. So does Queenie. Maybe Annie does too. How come I'm not so sure? I can't do that fancy April Powers stuff. If she's that good after being off sick, maybe I don't deserve MVP.

The whistle blasts, and I push forward into a wall of orange. *Oof.* I remember this feeling. They dig in hard against the concrete, and as much as I push I can barely move them forward. These girls must practice with Uptown, because they skate the same way. Low, strong and slow. *Come on, Robin, Annie's watching. Push hard. Trust your team. Let's go!*

My team? Oh, right, those amazing girls in purple shirts holding the other team's jammer back for me.

"Robin, inside!" Kat breaks away from her own wall to lay a big hit on the inside orange blocker and open up a hole for me. But the orange jammer sees it first and uses the opportunity to dart through. I follow her, and we break out of the pack together.

"Skate, Robin, skate!" Queenie yells from the bench. "You can beat her!"

I can? I *can!* I do a crossover and put on a burst of power, scooting around the orange jammer on her outside as she rounds the track toward the pack on her scoring pass.

"Call it! Call it!" her coach screams from the bench, but the jammer is too focused to notice, her ponytail swinging back and forth behind her as she moves sideways toward the pack. I push forward, and Kat knocks over two orange blockers at once, opening up another hole for me. I skate into the pack and pick up three points.

Whistles echo across the arena as the jam ends, and the jam refs raise their hands to send the points to the scorekeepers.

"With a slip-up on the part of Midtown's jammer, Creek City picks up three points without even getting lead, putting them ahead four points to one. But it's still anybody's game."

Jim the Announcer Guy is right. Next jam, April gets out after almost a minute of dancing back and forth to break up the pack and scores only two points, with their jammer slipping by for three.

"Can you go out again, Robin? I know we're asking you a lot." Queenie has held the jammer cover out to me more and more often. *Come on, Robin, you can do anything for an hour!*

"Yes, Coach!" I pick up a few points here and there, but Midtown is tough. They move together as a unit, and I can't break them apart. Right when I get out, their jammer escapes too. We can't put together a solid lead.

Usually Queenie can send April out every other jam, and we rely on her to rack up those twenty-point jams that set us out front in a game. With the way she's breathing hard after every jam, our team has turned to fielding pinch jammers just to get us through the game.

"Okay, Kat. Our jammers need to sit a couple out and rest up. I know you can do it!" Queen dangles the jammer cover in front of Kat, who never, ever jams. She sighs and pulls the elastic over her helmet.

"Okay, Coach, you got it. Just this once though." On the whistle Kat pushes hard and tries to pummel her way through the center of the pack, but she gets stuck behind an immovable defensive wall of orange. Their jammer laps her twice. She pries open a hole between two blockers and manages to escape, but the Midtown jammer calls the jam off, leaving her down nine points.

"With one jam to go, that's a lead change. Creek City has some catching up to do! This game could still go any direction! What a season finale this is!"

"All right, girls. I need to get my most experienced jammer out there. We're down by three, so we just need lead and one scoring pass to win." Queenie holds out the jammer cover. "Ready to win the game?"

Chapter Twenty-Three

April takes the jammer cover from Queenie and turns it over in her hands. "Yes, Coach. I'm ready to win this game." She brings the elastic cover up to her helmet, pauses and then holds it out in front of her instead.

"Robin, are you ready to earn those points for us?"

What? Is this really happening?

"What do you mean, April? Go out there and jump the apex. Win the game!" We're three points down, and Queenie gave *her* the jammer star. Annie is here to scout *her*. Not me. April is still and will always be the best. The MVP.

"No, Robin. You've got this. You've been picking up points all game. And, honestly, I'm exhausted. I know I've been tough on you, but you've been working hard, and it shows. I trust you. You can win this for us." She holds the jammer cover out to me.

"Queenie?" I look to Queenie for her usual no-nonsense approach. She couldn't possibly let April give me the jammer star *now* of all times.

"All right, jammer girl, you've got the star. Go show us what you've got." Queenie pushes the jammer cover into my hands. "Better get moving. Jam's about to start!"

On the jam line, my heart is in my stomach and my stomach is in my throat. *Come on, Robin, even April thinks you can do this. Annie's out there watching. Queenie's watching. April's watching. Let's make all that positive visualization a reality. Show them why you can be the MPV.*

"FIVE SECONDS!"

Scree!

I push into the center of the pack and wiggle as hard as I can against the orange wall in front of me.

"Hold her! She's moving toward the outside!"

"We've got their jammer, Robin, keep pushing!" Kat hollers from behind me. I'm moving their wall forward, almost far enough up that they'll have to let me go. I feel their blockers starting to ease up as my legs burn, pushing against them. We're all tired, but I have to keep going. Two more minutes. Four more points.

"No pack!" The referee's call forces the wall to release me, and I hear two whistles. Lead jammer! That's me!

A cheer roars through the crowd, and I hear Queenie and another voice yelling from the bench. "Go, Robin! You've got this! Four points and you're done!"

Is that April, cheering for me?

I race toward the pack, my crossovers smooth and efficient even as my legs ache.

One pass through this pack, and I can call it off and win the game! Their jammer is on her way back, but I've got time!

The orange wall is split, two blockers on each side. I blast down the center, hoping they won't reform before I get there. As they pull together to try to knock me down, I slip through the middle and tap my hands to my hips to end the jam. An orange blocker goes flying, and I hear the whistle blast. The end of the game? No, not enough whistles. A penalty.

"Purple, one three, low block!"

Purple, thirteen. No, wait, that's me! It can't be. I didn't—

As I sprint to the penalty box I realize I must have kicked that blocker's skate out as I burst into the pack. And now I'm headed for thirty seconds in the box while their jammer skates toward the pack on her scoring pass.

"That's an unlucky blow for Creek City as Robin CookieJars gets sent to the box on a low block just shy of calling it off and winning the game! Does Midtown have

enough time to score with ten seconds to go? Let's see."

The short girl with the ponytail bolts into the pack, moving to the inside, then to the outside and back in again, drawing our blockers with her. Kat just grazes her leg and almost knocks her out as she runs down the inside line. The final whistles blow to end the jam.

One long, sweeping whistle, and I'm still in the box as the game ends and the points rack up on the scoreboard.

"That's it, folks. It looks like Midtown Mini Mayhem has brought home the win by only three points. What a game!"

That familiar lump is rising in my throat. I can't even look at my bench. Queenie and April must be so mad. I couldn't do it. I couldn't win the game for us.

"Number thirteen, you can leave the box now. I think your coach is calling you!" The penalty-box official taps me on the shoulder, and I pull my face out of my hands, wiping the backs of my wristguards under my eyes.

"Sorry, what?"

"Robin! Robin!" Queenie waves me over to the bench. "Great job out there, jammer girl! Only three points. I'm not going to complain about a loss like that!"

"But I lost the game for us, Coach! I went to the box!"

"We lost the game together, but we played hard. It was an unlucky penalty, no big deal. You still did a great job. We relied on you, and you pulled through the whole game. Great work!" Queenie pulls the jammer cover off my helmet and cringes. "Yikes, this thing is sweaty. I'm going to need to do some laundry before next game!" She walks away holding the jammer cover at arm's length.

"Stick around, junior derby fans, because in just a few minutes, I will be announcing your season MVP!"

Oh yeah, MVPs. I wonder who—

"Hey, Robin, I need to talk to you for a minute."

It's April. And she wants to talk.

Chapter Twenty-Four

"I know you want to hear the MVP announcement, but—"

April Powers wants to talk to me after the game. She usually bolts straight for the change room. She must be regretting her decision to hand over the cover. We lost, and maybe she thinks it's my fault.

"Hi, April, I, um—"

"Listen, Robin, I know I haven't been the best teammate lately, especially not to you. I said some things that were super out of line, and I really shouldn't have. I didn't mean that you weren't a good skater or that you couldn't get MVP. I mean, I think you're a really great player. The way you push the pack is amazing."

Is this really coming out of April Powers's mouth? She thinks I'm a good skater?

"Aren't you mad I lost the game for us?"

"What? No way, you did great. I would have lost it by way more—trust me!" April laughs. "And you should be the one who is mad after how I treated you! Listen, you don't have to forgive me for everything I said and did. I mean, I probably wouldn't. It isn't an excuse, but I was going through a lot. I was struggling there for a while. I talked to Annie when she came to our practice and what she said really sank in with me. She even helped hook me up with some good resources and information. I don't know what would have happened if she hadn't come by..."

Does she know about my message to Annie? That I asked Annie if she would come help get through to April?

"I guess I was just lucky she decided to run a practice. I could have lost everything—

my derby, my school prospects, even the chance to go to prom, I guess."

The mic roars in the background, but I can't hear what Jim the Announcer Guy is saying. Something about teamwork, learning together, helping each other out as junior derby skaters.

"I guess what I'm saying," April continues, "is that I'm sorry. And thank you, Robin. I may have a few more trophies, but as far as I'm concerned, you're the real MVP."

I gulp back a different kind of lump rising in my throat as April raises her hand for a high five. "Team Jammer Star?"

"Team Jammer Star." Our wristguards clack together as the crowd erupts into a loud cheer.

"And tonight, as you remember, we are announcing our all-season MVP, the skater who made the biggest mark on the junior derby track this whole season. This year it comes from our winning team...

"Congratulations to Midtown Mini Mayhem jammer Smasherella!"

The girl with the ponytail skates forward as her teammates jump up and down on their toe-stops, cheering for her.

"Wooooo! Smasherella!" April cheers. I join her, clapping my wristguards loudly together. The girl hoists the all-season MVP trophy.

"Let's go congratulate her," April suggests. "She skated a great game." I nod, and we roll over to the announcer's table to high-five our new favorite junior jammer.

"Great job, Smasherella!" says April.

"You're really a tough one to catch!" I add.

"Thanks, you two!" Smash grins. "I want to know how you get so much power on that push, Robin! And that footwork, April—it's wicked! Want to chat at the after party? I hear there'll be pancakes!"

Concern flashes over April's face for a second, and then it's gone. "Sure!" she answers. "You in, Robin?"

"You bet!" I grin. "Didn't you know? The official after-party food of Team Jammer Star is pancakes!"

Chapter Twenty-Five

The Pancake Hut isn't going to let us in wearing stinky derby gear, so I dash after April to the change room to gear down. On the way there, we almost run full tilt into one of the volunteers pulling up the track barrier.

"Whoa, whoa, whoa, slow down there, speedy jammers!"

She stands up tall. Oh man, it's Annie Mossity. In all the cheering for Smash, I totally forgot she was here. By the look on April's face, she did too.

April picks her jaw off the floor enough to stammer, "Oh my god! I'm so sorry, Miss Mossity."

"No worries. I didn't expect to be making contact tonight, but I guess derby is always a contact sport, even for the volunteers." She laughs. "I was hoping to run into you two anyway, although maybe not so literally."

Annie unzips her track-jacket pocket and pulls out two folded pieces of paper. "Now that I'm not getting run over, here's what I was hoping to give you."

She hands us each a piece of paper with a calendar on it. The top of the printout reads *CREEK CITY ALL-STARS PRACTICE SCHEDULE.*

"You're April Powers, right? I hear you are about to age out of your league and might be looking for an adult team."

"Yeah! I turn eighteen next month." April's hands are shaking as she holds the schedule.

"Well, if you're interested, the Creek City All-Stars are starting our season practices next month, and we have a spot we'd like to fill. If you're interested, send us an email, and we'll get you the details. No tryout required after a strong performance like that."

April's jaw is back on the floor as she struggles to respond.

"I'll let you think on it for a while, no pressure." Annie grins. "As for you, Robin CookieJars, your coach Miss Queenie tells me I can't steal you away for the All-Stars just yet, but in a couple years' time, you are going to terrify all my adult skaters with that amazing push."

My ears must be bright red from how much I'm blushing. I can feel the heat in my face as I try to contain my smile.

"For now, keep a hold of that schedule, and if your parents are okay with it, we'd love to have you check out any of our non-contact practices. Make sure it doesn't get in the way of school or anything, but having a few more skaters out at endurance or skills practice only helps us out in the long run, and I think you've got what it takes to keep up."

Annie Mossity wants *me* to come to adult All-Star practice. Me. *Me!*

"Honestly, I don't know why I come to these junior games because you girls terrify me. You're going to be kicking my butt and beating up all my teammates in a couple years."

"Thank you! Thank you!" I blurt. I feel silly and giddy and am trying not to jump up and down on my skates. *Imagine! Annie Mossity being afraid of me?*

"Powers, CookieJars! You two coming or what? I thought jammers were supposed to be fast! Hurry up, slowpokes!"

"That Queenie doesn't have much patience for anyone, does she? Better get a move on if you're going to make it to the after party. Enjoy those pancakes. You earned them. See you at All-Stars practice, Jammer Stars!"

As soon as Annie turns and walks away, April and I both jump up and down on our toe-stops. "Can you believe it! Annie Mossity! *The* Annie Mossity!" I squeal.

"And you're going to play on her team! You're going to be on the Creek City All-Stars!"

April's smile covers her whole face. "I'm going to have to get so strong! I'm going to have to learn to push better! Robin, can you help me? I'll teach you footwork if you can help me move walls. Give me all your tips! What about that Super MVP Action Plan you mentioned at practice? The Creek City All-Stars. Holy crap!" April holds the schedule out in front of her. "Where do we even start?"

"Come on, jammers, gear down and let's go! The team is waiting!" Queenie calls.

I laugh. "It's going to be a lot of hard work. And a lot of fun," I tell April. "I think that means we start with pancakes."

Glossary

Apex jump: An advanced move in which a skater (usually a jammer) avoids blockers by jumping into the air at the "apex" or turn of the track and landing on the other side of the pack. This jump is not only a quick way of scoring points while avoiding hits, but also often a fan favorite.

Blocker: Most skaters on the track are blockers. Each team fields four blockers at a time (unless someone is in the penalty box!). Their job is to stop the other team's jammer from getting through the "pack." They also have to help their own jammer break through so that she can score points.

Bout: Another name for a roller-derby game. Bouts or games are broken up into two thirty-minute halves, and each half is made up of smaller jams.

Crossovers: Crossing one leg over the other while skating in order to be as powerful and efficient as possible. Skaters at all levels practice this move to improve their form and increase their speed.

Grand slam: When one jammer passes all four blockers on the other team as well as their jammer and scores all five possible points in one pass through the pack. Grand slams can quickly add up and can help a jammer earn twenty to thirty points in one jam.

Jam/power jam: Roller-derby bouts or games are broken up into segments called jams. Jams last a maximum of two minutes but can be as short as a few seconds if the lead jammer decides to "call off" or end the jam early. After every jam there is a thirty-second break so the teams can switch players. A power jam occurs when the opposing team's jammer is in the penalty box and is unable to score points.

Jammer: The skater who scores the points. Each team fields one jammer at a time.

You can spot them on the track because there is a star on each side of their helmet cover. A jammer scores a point for each opposing skater she passes.

Jammer cover: A stretchy, pull-on helmet cover with a star on each side to identify the jammer.

Lead jammer: The first jammer to push, spin or dodge her way out of the pack of blockers. She earns the advantage of being able to end or "call off" the jam at any time.

MVP: Most valuable player. In roller derby, it is common to see jammers and blockers receive separate MVP awards. Sometimes one MVP is announced for the entire game, or no MVPs are chosen at all!

Pack: The largest group of blockers, containing members of both teams, skating together on the track. Jammers fight to break through the pack in order to get lead-jammer status and score points.

Pivot: A blocker who also wears a special helmet cover, but with a stripe down its middle instead of a star on each side. Each team fields one pivot at a time. Pivots are the only blockers who can become jammers mid-jam through a move called a star pass. A jammer can hand off her star cover to the pivot, who then becomes the jammer.

Track: Roller derby is often played on an oval flat track (derby played on a banked track has different rules). Derby leagues tape a rope over the track boundary lines so that skaters can feel when they have skated out of bounds. Occasionally, the rope can take skaters by surprise, causing trips and falls.

Toe-stops: Toe-stops (or stoppers) are located on the front of quad roller skates. Derby players (especially jammers) don't just use them for stopping. They also run, jump, spin and do fancy footwork using their stoppers.

Acknowledgments

To the roller-derby skaters, officials, coaches, volunteers and fans I have met over the past eight years, thank you for sharing this amazing sport and for challenging me every day. I am consistently amazed by (and frankly terrified of) the junior skaters around the world taking roller derby to new levels.

Thank you to my editor, Tanya Trafford, for her keen eye and for making space for roller derby in the Orca Sports series. To Jen Cameron, Ella Collier and everyone at Orca Book Publishers, thank you for your work bringing *Jammer Star* into being.

Much appreciation also goes to Joe Mac for his wonderful cover photograph, which perfectly captures the action of derby, and to Drop Dead Alice for her tenacious jammer energy.

Thank you to Tanya Snyder at the Literary Press Group for encouraging me to write through my thoughts on roller derby and body image.

To all my friends and teammates who listened to plot ideas and brainstormed derby names with me, your expertise and creativity are much appreciated!

Thanks to my parents, Len and Jill, for watching countless derby games before they knew the rules, for always supporting my endeavors and for reading early versions of this manuscript.

And, of course, thanks to Oliver for the unwavering love and support and for tolerating me reading, re-writing and re-reading sections of *Jammer Star* out loud over and over without complaint.

Finally, thank you, reader! I hope you enjoy all the hits, jumps and spills!

This project was generously supported by the City of Windsor's Arts, Culture and Heritage Fund.

Kate Hargreaves (aka Pain Eyre) is a writer, book designer and roller-derby skater. She is the author of *Talking Derby: Stories from a Life on Eight Wheels* and *Leak*, a collection of poems. She lives in Windsor, Ontario, where she helped found the city's roller-derby league in 2010. When she's not working as an academic writing adviser, she spends her time writing, cycling with her husband and cuddling with Winn the cat.

orca sports

For more information on all the books
in the Orca Sports series, please visit
orcabook.com.